Chelsea
& The
New Puppy

Story by Loren Spiotta-DiMare
Illustrated by Kara Lee

 Town Book Press
Westfield, New Jersey

Town Book Press
255 East Broad Street
Westfield, NJ 07090

Printed in Korea

10 9 8 7 6 5 4 3 2 1

Library of Congress Cataloging-in-Publication Data
Spiotta-DiMare, Loren.
    Chelsea & the new puppy / story by Loren Spiotta-DiMare ; illustrated by Kara Lee.
        p. cm.
Summary: Chelsea, a six-year-old Welsh springer spaniel who is accustomed to being
the only dog in the family, has a difficult time when her owners bring home an assertive
field spaniel puppy.
ISBN 1-892657-03-1
1. Spaniels--Juvenile fiction. [1. Spaniels--Fiction. 2. Dogs--Fiction. 3.
Animals--Infancy--Fiction.] I. Title: Chelsea and the new puppy. II. Lee, Kara, 1964- ill.
III. Title.

PZ10.3.S679 Ch 2001
[E]--dc21
                                                                    2001035561

For Chelsea and Smokey, of course.
                    L.S~D

In loving memory of my son, Jordan,
        my little angel in heaven.
                    K.L.

"A puppy will be good company for Chelsea," Mom said. Maybe she's referring to a visitor I thought, perking my ears to catch every word. "And, she'll have a friend to play with when she's older," Dad added.

ANOTHER DOG! I dropped my head onto my paws and sighed. No one asked how I felt about it. Mom and Dad were all the company I needed.

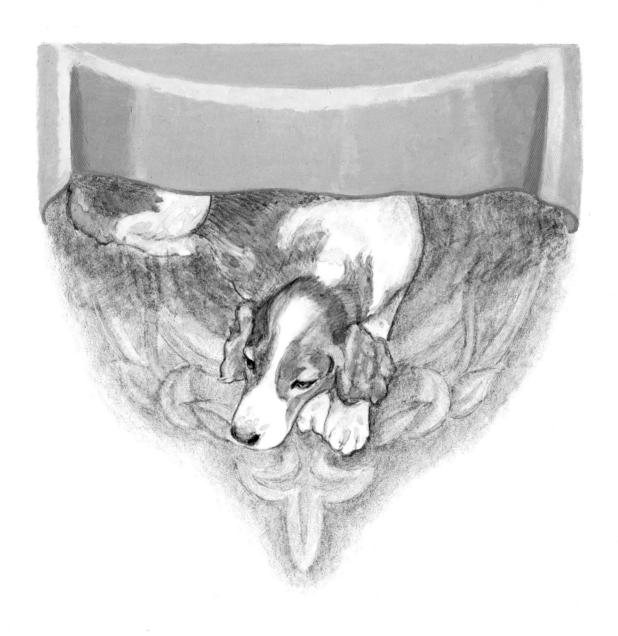

I watched Dad pull my old crate out of the basement. I hadn't seen it in years. Then I noticed a new leash and collar, and two new dog bowls.

Mom and Dad packed the crate into the car. They said goodbye and promised to be back soon. I kept hoping they would change their minds about the puppy.

When Dad came home it was getting dark. He grabbed my leash. I was so excited I danced around his feet.

Once we stepped outside, it began to rain. I hate to get wet but Dad insisted we walk. He brought me to the park. I saw Mom standing under an umbrella. As I strained at my leash to reach her, I realized she wasn't alone.

A big, chocolate brown puppy stood next to her. He was nearly as tall as me. He wanted to play. I ignored him and stretched up on my hind legs to greet Mom.

Mom and Dad brought us home. The puppy dashed from room to room. He jumped on the couch. I barked at him. Then he hopped onto the coffee table. "Off!" Mom scolded.

Dad sat in our leather chair drinking a glass of water. "We have to think of a name for the puppy," Mom said. "He's barreling around here like a bear cub. Why don't we call him, Smokey Bear?" Dad replied. Mom agreed.

Just then Smokey snatched Dad's drink off
the table and bounded off with it.

We all chased him.

Dad gently took the glass away. Luckily it didn't break. Mom and Dad started to laugh. Not me. The new puppy already caused more trouble than I ever had. I wished they would take him back. But it only got worse.

When Mom works, I like to sleep under her desk. The first time Smokey saw me there, he ran in and pushed me aside. I snarled, but he wouldn't move.

So I sat on a chair in the corner of the room. Mom tried to coax me off. But I wouldn't budge.

At night, Smokey stole my dinner. I growled to keep him
away. He ignored me. Mom had to stand guard over us.

I had some favorite toys. When someone threw my
plastic pickle, Smokey chased it too. If I got there
first, he'd snatch it out of my mouth. Sometimes
when he had his own toy, he'd still take mine
and prance around with both.

After awhile playing wasn't fun anymore,
so I stopped. But I wouldn't give up
my towel no matter what. I hung
on with all my might.

At bedtime, I heard Mom and Dad talking about me. "Chelsea isn't happy about the new puppy," Mom said. "She's always moping."

"It's going to take time," Dad replied, "She's still adjusting and Smokey is very pushy."

"I guess so. I hope you're right." Mom's voice drifted off.

Mom began to take me out alone. We went for rides in the car and runs in the park. It was just like the old days. She also encouraged me to play with Smokey. But he only grew bigger and rougher.

When we were let loose in our enclosed yard he became so excited he knocked me over racing through the door. After a few times I was afraid to go with him. I was always afraid.

Dad tried to comfort me. I sat in his lap as he massaged my neck and rubbed my ears. I was so comfortable. Then Smokey leaped into the chair and pushed me off. That did it–I crawled away to hide.

"Chelsea, come here, it's okay," Mom called.

"Here, girl. Don't be scared," Dad echoed.

I pretended not to hear.

"Where is she?   Did you look under the bed?"
Mom was getting frantic.

"Maybe she slipped outside," Dad said.

I squeezed behind the washing machine.

"Chelsea, Chelsea, where are you?" Mom cried. I was stuck and started to whimper. I could hear Mom and Dad but they couldn't hear me. I began to howl. But no one came.

I wiggled and squirmed. I scratched at the floor. But I couldn't get out.

Suddenly, Smokey was there. He pawed at me and barked loudly. I was relieved to see him. He kept barking, pawing and wagging his tail.

"What's wrong with Smokey? This is no time to play. We have to find Chelsea," I heard Mom say.

Smokey's barking grew louder and louder. I heard footsteps running down the basement stairs. "Stop that, Smokey!" Dad reprimanded.

"Smokey, come," Mom called. He ignored her. I started to bark too.

"It's Chelsea," Dad cried out. "Smokey found her!" He pulled the washing machine away from the wall and I jumped out. We all hugged and kissed. Smokey even yodeled.

Now Smokey and I are best friends. He tries to be gentle and we're always side by side. When Mom's working, we sleep under her desk together. At night, even though we have our own beds, we curl up on mine.

I'm never lonely if Mom and Dad are away because Smokey is with me. I like to lie on the center hall steps. From that spot I can see out the front window and watch our neighborhood. Smokey is too big to fit on a step, but he rests on the floor at the bottom of the stairs. We guard the house together.

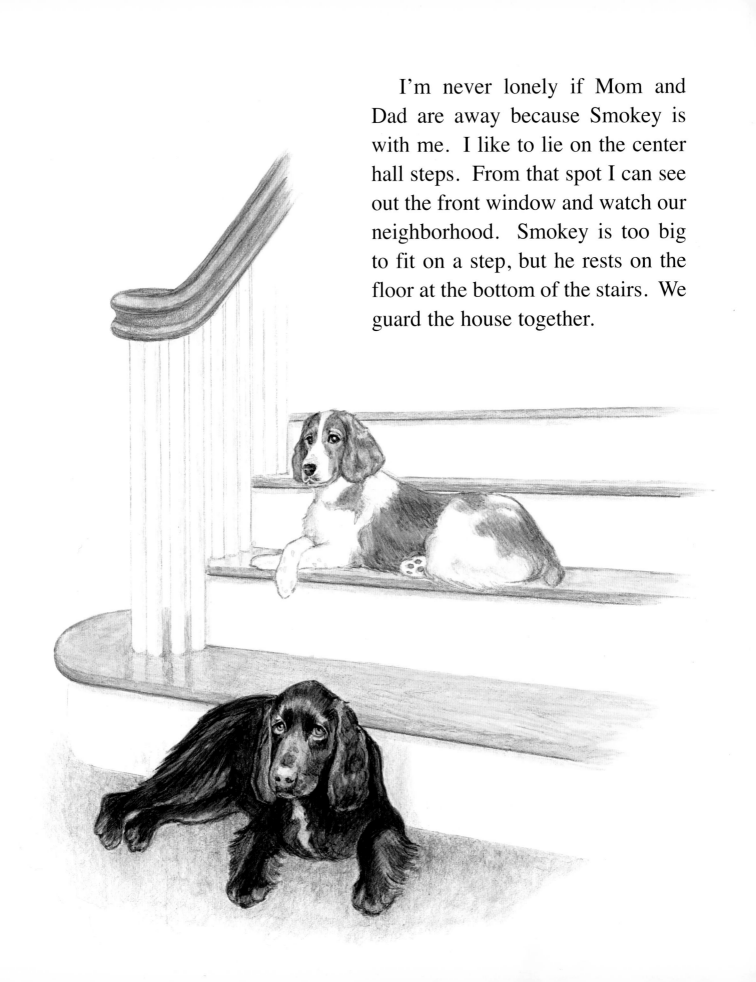

Still, we are happiest when Mom and Dad come home. As soon as we hear their car, we race each other to the window. When they wave, we leap off the window box, run between the couches and greet them at the back door.

Mom snaps on our collars. Dad grabs the leashes.
Then the four of us head for the park together.